THE CELEBRATED JUMPING FROG OF CALAVERAS COUNTY

AND

THE £1,000,000 BANK NOTE

THE CELEBRATED JUMPING FROG OF CALAVERAS COUNTY

AND

THE £1,000,000 BANK NOTE

MARK TWAIN

A SAMUEL CLEMENS BOOK

A SAMUEL CLEMENS BOOK

www.wildsidepress.com

CONTENTS

THE CELEBRATED JUMPING FROG OF CALAVERAS COUNTY

In compliance with the request of a friend of mine, who wrote me from the East, I called on good-natured, garrulous old Simon Wheeler, and inquired after my friend's friend, *Leonidas W.* Smiley, as requested to do, and I hereunto append the result. I have a lurking suspicion that *Leonidas W.* Smiley is a myth; that my friend never knew such a personage; and that he only conjectured that, if I asked old Wheeler about him, it would remind him of his infamous *Jim* Smiley, and he would go to work and bore me nearly to death with some infernal reminiscence of him as long and tedious as it should be useless for me. If that was the design, it certainly succeeded.

I found Simon Wheeler dozing comfortably by the bar-room stove of the old, dilapidated tavern in the ancient mining camp of Angel's, and I noticed that he was fat and bald-headed, and had an expression of winning gentleness and simplicity upon his tranquil countenance. He roused up and gave me good-day. I told him a friend of mine had commissioned me to make some inquiries about a cherished companion of his boyhood named *Leonidas W.* Smiley—*Rev. Leonidas W.* Smiley—a young minister of the Gospel, who he had heard was at one time a resident of Angel's Camp. I added that, if Mr. Wheeler could tell me any thing about this Rev. Leonidas W. Smiley, I would feel under many obligations to him.

Simon Wheeler backed me into a corner and blockaded me there with his chair, and then sat me down and reeled off the monotonous narrative which follows this paragraph. He never smiled, he never frowned, he never changed his voice from the gentle-flowing key to which he tuned the initial sentence, he never betrayed the slightest suspicion of enthusiasm; but all through the interminable narrative there ran a vein of impressive earnestness and sincerity, which showed me plainly that, so far from his imagining that there was any thing ridiculous or funny about his story, he regarded it as a really important matter, and admired its two heroes as men of transcendent genius in *finesse*. To me, the spectacle of a man drifting serenely along through such a queer yarn without ever smiling, was exquisitely absurd. As I said before, I asked him to tell me what he knew of Rev. Leonidas W. Smiley, and he replied as follows. I let him go on in his own way, and never interrupted him once:

There was a feller here once by the name of *Jim* Smiley, in the winter of '49—or may be it was the spring of '50—I don't recollect exactly, somehow, though what makes me think it was one or the other is because I remember the big flume wasn't finished when he first came to the camp; but any way he was the curiosest man about always betting on any thing that turned up you ever see, if he could get anybody to bet on the other side; and if he couldn't, he'd change sides. Any way that suited the other man would suit him—any way just so's he got a bet, *he* was satisfied. But still he was lucky, uncommon lucky; he most always come out winner. He was always ready and laying for a chance; there couldn't be no solitry thing mentioned but that feller'd offer to bet on it, and take any side you please, as I was just telling you. If there was a horse-race, you'd find him flush, or you'd find him busted at the end of it; if there was a dog-fight, he'd bet on it; if there was a cat-fight, he'd bet on it; if there was a chicken-fight, he'd bet on it; why, if there was two birds sitting on a fence, he would bet you which one would fly first; or if there was a camp-meeting, he would be there reg'lar, to bet on Parson Walker, which he judged to be the best exhorter about here, and so he was, too, and a good man. If he even seen a straddle-bug start to go anywheres, he would bet you how long it would take him to get wherever he was going to, and if you took him up, he would foller that straddle-bug to Mexico but what he would find out where he was bound for and how long he was on the road. Lots of the boys here has seen that Smiley, and can tell you about him. Why, it never made no difference to *him*—he would bet on *any* thing—the dangdest feller. Parson Walker's wife laid very sick once, for a good while, and it seemed as if they warn't going to save her; but one morning he come in, and Smiley asked how she was, and he said she was considerable better—thank the Lord for his inf'nit mercy—and coming on so smart that, with the blessing of Prov'dence, she'd get well yet; and Smiley, before he thought, says, "Well, I'll risk two-and-a-half that she don't, any way."

This-yer Smiley had a mare—the boys called her the fifteen-minute nag, but that was only in fun, you know, because, of course, she was faster than that—and he used to win money on that horse, for all she was so slow and always had the asthma, or the distemper, or the consumption, or something of that kind. They used to give her two or three hundred yards start, and then pass her under way; but always at the fag-end of the race she'd get excited and desperate-like, and come cavorting and straddling up, and scattering her legs around limber, sometimes in the air, and sometimes out to one side amongst the fences, and kicking up m-o-r-e dust, and raising m-o-r-e racket with her coughing and sneezing and blowing her nose—and always fetch up at the stand just about a neck ahead, as near as you could cipher it down.

And he had a little small bull pup, that to look at him you'd think he wan't worth a cent, but to set around and look ornery, and lay for a chance to steal something. But as soon as the money was up on him, he was a different dog; his under-jaw'd begin to stick out like the fo'castle of a steamboat, and his teeth would uncover, and shine savage like the furnaces. And a dog might tackle him, and bully-rag him, and bite him, and throw him over his shoulder two or three times, and Andrew Jackson—which was the name of the pup—Andrew Jackson would never let on but what *he* was satisfied, and hadn't expected nothing else—and the bets being doubled and doubled on the other side all the time, till the money was all up; and then all of a sudden he would grab that other dog jest by the j'int of his hind leg and freeze to it—not chaw, you understand, but only jest grip and hang on till they throwed up the sponge, if it was a year. Smiley always come out winner on that pup, till he harnessed a dog once that didn't have no hind legs, because they'd been sawed off by a circular saw, and when the thing had gone along far enough, and the money was all up, and he come to make a snatch for his pet holt, he saw in a minute how he'd been imposed on, and how the other dog had him in the door, so to speak, and he 'peared surprised, and then he looked sorter discouraged-like, and didn't try no more to win the fight, and so he got shucked out bad. He give Smiley a look, as much as to say his heart was broke, and it was *his* fault, for putting up a dog that hadn't no hind legs for him to take holt of, which was his main dependence in a fight, and then he limped off a piece and laid down and died. It was a good pup, was that Andrew Jackson, and would have made a name for hisself if he'd lived, for the stuff was in him, and he had genius—I know it, because he hadn't had no opportunities to speak of, and it don't stand to reason that a dog could make such a fight as he could under them circumstances, if he hadn't no talent. It always makes me feel sorry when I think of that last fight of his'n, and the way it turned out.

Well, this-yer Smiley had rat-tarriers, and chicken cocks, and tom-cats, and all them kind of things, till you couldn't rest, and you couldn't fetch nothing for him to bet on but he'd match you. He ketched a frog one day, and took him home, and said he cal'klated to edercate him; and so he never done nothing for three months but set in his back yard and learn that frog to jump. And you bet you he *did* learn him, too. He'd give him a little punch behind, and the next minute you'd see that frog whirling in the air like a doughnut—see him turn one summerset, or may be a couple, if he got a good start, and come down flat-footed and all right, like a cat. He got him up so in the matter of catching flies, and kept him in practice so constant, that he'd nail a fly every time as far as he could see him. Smiley said all a frog wanted was education, and he could do most any thing—and I believe him. Why, I've seen him set Dan'l Webster down here on this floor—Dan'l Webster was the name of the frog—and sing out, "Flies, Dan'l, flies!" and quicker'n you could wink, he'd spring straight up, and snake a fly off'n the counter there, and flop down on the floor again as solid as a gob of mud, and fall to scratching the side of his head with his hind foot as indifferent as if he hadn't no idea he'd been doin' any more'n any frog might do. You never see a frog so modest and straight-for'ard as he was, for all he was so gifted. And when it come to fair and square jumping on a dead level, he could get over more ground at one straddle than any animal of his breed you ever see. Jumping on a dead level was his strong suit, you understand; and when it come to that, Smiley would ante up money on him as long as he had a red. Smiley was monstrous proud of his frog, and well he might be, for fellers that had travelled and been everywheres, all said he laid over any frog that ever *they* see.

Well, Smiley kept the beast in a little lattice box, and he used to fetch him down town sometimes and lay for a bet. One day a feller—a stranger in the camp, he was—come across him with his box, and says,

"What might it be that you've got in the box?"

And Smiley says, sorter indifferent like, "It might be a parrot, or it might be a canary, may be, but it ain't—it's only just a frog."

And the feller took it, and looked at it careful, and turned it round this way and that, and says, "H'm—so't is. Well, what's *he* good for?"

"Well," Smiley says, easy and careless, "he's good enough for *one* thing, I should judge—he can out-jump ary frog in Calaveras county."

The feller took the box again, and took another long, particular look, and give it back to Smiley, and says, very deliberate, "Well, I don't see no p'ints about that frog that's any better'n any other frog."

"May be you don't," Smiley says. "May be you understand frogs, and may be you don't understand 'em; may be you've had experience, and may be you ain't, only a amature, as it were. Any ways, I've got *my* opinion, and I'll risk forty dollars that he can out-jump any frog in Calaveras county."

And the feller studied a minute, and then says, kinder sad like, "Well, I'm only a stranger here, and I ain't got no frog; but if I had a frog, I'd bet you."

And then Smiley says, "That's all right—that's all right—if you'll hold my box a minute, I'll go and get you a frog." And so the feller took the box, and put up his forty dollars along with Smiley's, and set down to wait.

So he set there a good while thinking and thinking to hisself, and then he got the frog out and prized his mouth open and took a teaspoon and filled him full of quail shot—filled him pretty near up to his chin—and set him on the floor. Smiley he went to the swamp and slopped around in the mud for a long time, and finally he ketched a frog, and fetched him in, and give him to this feller, and says:

"Now, if you're ready, set him alongside of Dan'l, with his fore-paws just even with Dan'l, and I'll give the word." Then he says, "One—two—three—jump!" and him and the feller touched up the frogs from behind, and the new frog hopped off, but Dan'l give a heave, and hysted up his shoulders—so—like a Frenchman, but it wan't no use—he couldn't budge; he was planted as solid as an anvil, and he couldn't no more stir than if he was anchored out. Smiley was a good deal surprised, and he was disgusted too, but he didn't have no idea what the matter was, of course.

The feller took the money and started away; and when he was going out at the door, he sorter jerked his thumb over his shoulders—this way—at Dan'l, and says again, very deliberate, "Well, I don't see no pints about that frog that's any better'n any other frog."

Smiley he stood scratching his head and looking down at Dan'l a long time, and at last he says, "I do wonder what in the nation that frog throw'd off for—I wonder if there ain't some thing the matter with him—he 'pears to look mighty baggy, somehow." And he ketched Dan'l by the nap of the neck, and lifted him up and says, "Why, blame my cats, if he don't weigh five pound!" and turned him upside down, and he belched out a double handful of shot. And then he see how it was, and he was the maddest man—he set the frog down and took out after that feller, but he never ketched him. And—

(Here Simon Wheeler heard his name called from the front yard, and got up to see what was wanted.) And turning to me as he moved away, he said: "Just set where you are, stranger, and rest easy—I an't going to be gone a second."

But, by your leave, I did not think that a continuation of the history of the enterprising vagabond *Jim* Smiley would be likely to afford me much information concerning the Rev. *Leonidas W.* Smiley, and so I started away.

At the door I met the sociable Wheeler returning, and he buttonholed me and recommenced:

"Well, this-yer Smiley had a yaller one-eyed cow that didn't have no tail, only just a short stump like a bannanner, and—"

"Oh, hang Smiley and his afflicted cow!" I muttered, good-naturedly, and bidding the old gentleman good-day, I departed.

THE £1,000,000 BANK NOTE

CHAPTER ONE

From San Francisco to London

When I was 27 years old, I worked in an office in San Francisco. I did my job well and my future was promising. I was alone in the world and I was happy.

On Saturday afternoons I didn't work. I sailed my little sailboat on San Francisco Bay. One Saturday afternoon, I sailed out too far. The strong afternoon wind pushed my sailboat out of the bay, into the Pacific Ocean.

That night, when I had lost all hope, a small British brig saw me and took me on board. The brig was sailing to London. The voyage was long and stormy. I worked as a sailor to pay for my trip.

When I arrived in London, my clothes were old and dirty. I had only one dollar in my pocket. With this dollar, I ate and slept for the first twenty-four hours. During the next twenty-four hours, I didn't eat and didn't sleep.

At about ten o'clock the following morning, I went to Portland Place. I saw a child walking past, holding a big pear. The child ate one small piece and then threw the pear onto the street.

I stopped and looked at it.

I was very hungry and I really wanted that pear. But every time I tried to get it, someone passed by and looked at me. I quickly turned in the other direction and waited for the person to pass by. I tried again and again to get that pear, but the same thing happened. I was desperate. I decided to get the pear and not to worry about the people who saw me. At that moment, a gentleman opened a window behind me and said, "Come in here, please."

A well-dressed servant opened the door. He took me to a beautiful room.

Here, two old gentlemen were sitting and discussing something important.

Their breakfast was on the table. I was very hungry and I stared at their breakfast.

I want to tell the reader that the two gentlemen had made a bet several days before. I knew nothing about the bet until later. Let me tell you what happened.

CHAPTER TWO

An Unusual Bet

The two old gentlemen were brothers. For several days, they argued about a very strange subject. They decided to end their argument with a bet, as the English usually do. The following was the subject of the bet.

The Bank of England issued two banknotes of a million dollars each for a public transaction with a foreign country. England used one banknote and the other remained in the bank.

At this point, Brother A said to Brother B, "If an honest and intelligent stranger arrives in London without a friend and without money, except for the $1,000,000 banknote, he will starve to death."

Brother B answered, "No! I don't agree."

Brother A said, "If he goes to the bank or anywhere else to change this big note, the police will put him in prison. Everyone will think he stole it."

They continued arguing for days, until Brother B said, "I'll bet $20,000 that the stranger will live for thirty days with the banknote and not go to prison."

Brother A accepted the bet. He went to the bank and bought the $1,000,000 banknote. After, he returned home and prepared a letter. Then the two brothers sat by the window and waited for the right man for the bet.

They saw a lot of honest faces go by, but they were not intelligent enough. Several faces were intelligent, but they were not honest. A lot of faces were honest and intelligent, but they were not poor enough. Other faces were honest, intelligent and poor, but they were not strangers.

When they saw me from the window, they thought I was the right man. They asked me questions, and soon they knew my story. Finally, they told me I was the right man for the bet. I asked them to explain the bet. One of the gentlemen gave me an envelope. I wanted to open it, but he said, "No, don't open it now. Wait until you are in your hotel room. Then read it very carefully."

I was confused and I wanted to discuss the subject with them. But they didn't. I felt hurt because I was the subject of a joke.

When I left their house, I looked for the pear on the street. It was gone. I was quite angry with those two gentlemen.

Far from their house, I opened the envelope. I saw that there was money inside! I didn't stop to read their letter.

I ran to the nearest eating place. I ate and ate and ate. At last, I took out the envelope with the money, to pay for my meal. I looked at the banknote and almost fainted. It was a banknote worth five million dollars!

I was speechless. I stared at the banknote. The two gentlemen had made a big mistake.

They probably wanted to give me a one-dollar banknote.

I saw the owner of the eating place staring at the banknote, too. We were both surprised. I did not know what to do or say. So, I simply gave him the note and said, "Give me the change, please."

The owner apologized a thousand times.

"I'm very sorry, but I can't change this banknote, sir."

"I don't have any other money. Please change this note." The owner then said, "You can pay for this food whenever you want, sir. I understand that you are a very rich gentleman. You like playing jokes on people by dressing like a poor man. You can come here and eat all you want, whenever you want. You can pay me when you want."

CHAPTER THREE

The Letter

When I arrived, the same servant opened the door. I asked for the two gentlemen.

"They are gone," the servant said.

"Gone? Gone where?"

"Oh, on a journey."

"But, where did they go?"

"To the Continent, I think."

"The Continent?"

There were no signature, no address, no date on the letter.

How strange! I didn't know what to think. I went to a park, sat down and thought about what to do. After an hour, I reached the decision that follows.

The two old gentlemen are playing a game that I don't understand. They are betting on me. (But, at that time, I didn't know anything about the details of the bet.)

If I go to the Bank of England to return the banknote, the bank will ask me lots of questions. If I tell the truth, no one will believe me. They will put me in an asylum. If I tell a lie, the police will put me in prison. I can't even give it to anyone, because no honest person will want it.

I can do only one thing: I must keep the bill for a whole month. And, I must not lose it. If I help the old man to win his bet, he will give me the job I want.

The idea of an important job with a big salary made me happy. With this exciting idea in mind, I began walking down the streets of London.

CHAPTER FOUR

At the Tailor's

Every time I passed in front of a tailor's, I wanted to enter and buy some new clothes.

But, I had no money to pay for them. The $1,000,000 banknote in my pocket was useless!

I passed in front of the same tailor's six times. At last I entered. I quietly asked if they had an old, unattractive suit that no one wanted to buy. The man I spoke to nodded his head, but he didn't speak. Then another man looked at me and nodded his head. I went to him and he said, "One moment, please."

After some time, he took me to a back room. He looked at several ugly suits that no one wanted. He chose the worst for me. I really wanted a suit, so I said nothing.

It was time to pay. "Can you wait a few days for the money? I haven't got any small change with me."

The man said, "Oh, you haven't? Well, I thought gentlemen like you carried large change."

"My friend," I replied, "you can't judge a stranger by the clothes he wears. I can pay for this suit. But, can you change a large banknote?"

"Oh, of course we can change a large banknote," he said coldly.

I gave him the banknote. He received it with a smile, a big smile that covered his face. When he read the banknote, his smile disappeared. The owner of the shop came over and asked me, "What's the trouble?"

"There isn't any trouble. I'm waiting for my change."

"Come, come. Give him his change, Tod. Quickly!"

Tod answered, "It's easy to say, but look at the banknote." The owner looked at the banknote. Then he looked at my package with the ugly suit.

"Tod," he shouted, "you are stupid! How can you sell this unattractive suit to a millionaire! Tod, you can't see the difference between a millionaire and a poor man."

"I apologize, sir," the owner continued. "Please take off those things you are wearing and throw them in the fire. Put on this fine shirt and this handsome suit. It's perfect for you—simple but elegant."

I told him I was very happy with the new suit.

"Oh, wait until you see what we can make for you in your size!

Tod, bring a pen and a book. Let me measure your leg, your arm…"

I didn't have a moment to speak.

The owner measured me. Then he ordered his tailors to make me morning suits, evening suits, shirts, coats and other things.

"But, my dear sir," I said, "I can order all these things only if you change my banknote. Or, if you can wait a while before I pay you."

"Wait a while. I'll wait forever, that's the word. Tod, send these things to the gentleman's address. Let the less important customers wait!

What's your address, sir?"

"I'm changing my home. I'll come back and give you my new address," I replied.

"Quite right, sir, quite right. Let me show you to the door, sir. Good day, sir, good day."

CHAPTER FIVE

The Poor Millionaire

The impossible happened. I bought everything I wanted without money. I showed my banknote and asked for change, but every time the same thing happened. No one was able to change it.

I bought all that I needed and all the luxuries that I wanted. I stayed at an expensive hotel in Hanover Square. I always had dinner at the hotel. But I preferred having breakfast at Harris's simple eating place. Harris's was the first place where I had a good meal with my million-dollar note. That's where it all started.

The news about me and my banknote was all over London.

Harris's eating place became famous because I had breakfast there. Harris was happy with all his new customers.

I lived like a rich, important man. I had money to spend. I lived in a dream. But often, I said to myself, "Remember, this dream will end when the two men return to London. Everything will change."

My story was in the newspapers. Everyone talked about the "strange millionaire with the million-dollar note in his pocket." Punch magazine drew a funny picture of me on the front page. People talked about everything I did and about everything I said. They followed me in the streets.

I kept my old clothes, and sometimes I wore them. It was fun when the shop owners thought I was poor. Then I showed them the banknote, and, oh, how their faces changed!

After ten days in London, I went to visit the American Ambassador. He was very happy to meet me. He invited me to a dinner-party that evening. He told me that he knew my father from Yale University. He invited me to visit his home whenever I wanted.

I was glad to have a new, important friend. I thought to myself, "I'll need an important friend, when the story of the million-dollar note and bet comes out."

I want the reader to know that I planned to pay back all the shop owners who sold me things on credit. "If I win the bet for the old gentleman," I thought, "I will have an important job. With an important job, I will have a big salary." I planned to pay back everyone with my first year's salary.

CHAPTER SIX

The Dinner Party

There were fourteen people at the dinner party. The Duke and Duchess of Shoreditch, and their daughter, Lady Anne-Grace-Eleanor de Bohun, the Earl and Countess of Newgate, Viscount Cheapside, Lord and Lady Blatherskite, the Ambassador and his wife and daughter, and some other people. There was also a beautiful, twenty-two-year old English girl, named Portia Langham. I fell in love with her in two minutes, and she with me!

After a while, the house servant presented another guest, Mr Lloyd Hastings. When Mr Hastings saw me, he said, "I think I know you."

"Yes, you probably do."

"Are you the—the—"

"Yes, I'm the strange millionaire with the million-dollar note in his pocket!"

"Well, well, this is a surprise. I never thought you were the same Henry Adams from San Francisco! Six months ago, you were working in the offices of Blake Hopkins in San Francisco. I remember clearly. You had a very small salary. And, at night, you helped me arrange the papers for the Gould and Curry Mining Company. Now you're a millionaire, a celebrity here in London. I can't believe it! How exciting!"

"I can't believe it, either, Lloyd."

"Just three months ago, we went to the Miner's Restaurant—"

"No, no, it was the What Cheer Restaurant."

"Right, it was the What Cheer. We went there at two o'clock in the morning. We had steak and coffee. That night we worked for six long hours on the Gould and Curry Mining Company papers. Do you remember, Henry, I asked you to come to London with me. I wanted you to help me sell the Gould and Curry gold mine shares. But you refused."

"Of course I remember. I didn't want to leave my job in San Francisco. And, I still think it's difficult to sell shares of a California gold mine here in London."

"You were right, Henry. You were so right. It is impossible to sell these shares here in London. My plan failed and I spent all my money. I don't want to talk about it."

"But you must talk about it. When we leave the dinner party, you must tell me what happened."

"Oh, can I? I really need to talk to a friend," Lloyd said, with water in his eyes.

"Yes, I want to hear the whole story, every word of it."

"Thank you, Henry. You're a true friend."

At this point, it was time for dinner. Thanks to the English system of precedence, there was no dinner.

The Duke of Shoreditch wanted to sit at the head of the table. The American Ambassador also wanted to sit at the head of the table. It was impossible for them to decide, so we had no dinner.

The English know about the system of precedence.

They have dinner before going out to dinner. But strangers know nothing about it. They remain hungry all evening.

Instead, we had a dish of sardines and a strawberry. Now it was time for everyone to play a game called cribbage. The English never play a game for fun. They play to win or to lose something.

Miss Langham and I played the game, but with little interest. I looked at her beautiful face and said, "Miss Langham, I love you!"

"Mr Adams," she said softly and smiled, "I love you too!"

This was a wonderful evening. Miss Langham and I were very happy. We smiled, laughed and talked.

I was honest with her. I told her that I was poor and that I didn't have a cent in the world. I explained that the million-dollar note was not mine. She was very curious to know more. I told her the whole story from the start. She laughed and laughed. She thought the story was very funny. I didn't understand why it was funny. I also explained that I needed an important job with a big salary to pay all my debts.

"Portia, dear, can you come with me on the day I must meet those two gentlemen?

"Well, yes, if I can help you," she replied.

"Of course you can help me. You are so lovely that when the two gentlemen see you, I can ask for any job and any salary. With you there, my sweet Portia, the two gentlemen won't refuse me anything."

CHAPTER SEVEN

A Million-Dollar Idea

At the end of the dinner party, I returned to the hotel with Hastings. He talked about his problems, but I didn't listen to him. I was thinking about Portia the whole time.

When we arrived at the hotel, Hastings said, "Let me just stand here and look at this marvelous hotel. It's a palace! What expensive furniture! You have everything you want. You are rich, Henry. And I am poor."

His words scared me. I, too, was poor. I didn't have a cent in the world, and I had debts to pay. I needed to win the gentleman's bet. This was my last hope. Hastings didn't know the truth.

"Henry, just a tiny part of your income can save me. I'm desperate!" Hastings cried.

"My dear Hastings, sit down here and drink this hot whiskey. Now tell me your whole story, every word of it."

"Do you want to hear my story again?"

"But, you never told me your story."

"Of course I told you my story, as we walked to the hotel. Don't you remember?"

"I didn't hear one word of it."

"Henry, are you ill? Is something wrong with you? What did you drink at the dinner party?"

"Oh, Hastings, I'm in love! I can only think about my sweet Portia. This is why I didn't hear your story before."

Hastings got up from his chair, shook my hand and laughed. "I'm very happy for you, Henry, very happy," he said smiling. "I'll tell you the whole story again." So he sat down and patiently started to tell me his story.

To make a long story short, the owners of the Gould and Curry Gold Mine sent Lloyd to England, to sell the shares of the mine for one million dollars. Any money he received over one million dollars was his to keep. Hastings's dream was to sell the shares for more than one million dollars, and become rich. He had only one month to sell the shares. He had done everything to sell them, but nobody wanted to buy them.

Then he jumped up and cried, "Henry, you can help me! Will you do it?"

"Tell me how."

"Give me a million dollars and I'll sell you all the shares. You will be the new owner of the gold mine. Don't, don't refuse."

I did not know what to say. I wanted to tell Hastings the truth. But then, an intelligent idea came to me. I thought about it for a moment and then calmly said, "I will save you, Lloyd."

"Then I am already saved! How can I thank you—"

"Let me finish, Lloyd. I will save you, but not in that way. I have a better way. I know everything about that mine. I know its great value. You will sell the shares by using my name. You can send anyone to me, since people in London know me. I will guarantee the gold mine. In a week or two, you will sell the shares for three million dollars, by using my name. And we'll share the money you earn. Half to you and half to me." Lloyd was very happy and excited. He danced around the room and laughed.

"I can use your name! Your name—think of it. The rich Londoners will run to buy these shares. I'm saved! And I'll never forget you, Henry!"

CHAPTER EIGHT

Back to Portland Place

The next day, all of London talked about the shares of the California gold mine. I stayed in my hotel and said to everyone who came to me, "Yes, I know Mr Hastings. He's a very honest man. And I know the gold mine, because I lived in the California Gold Country. It is a mine of great value." People were now interested in buying the shares.

I spent every evening with Portia at the American Ambassador's house. I didn't tell her about the shares and the mine. It was a surprise. We talked about our love and our future together.

Finally, the end of the month arrived. Lots of rich Londoners bought the shares of the mine. I had a million dollars of my own in the London and County Bank. And Lloyd did too.

It was time to meet with the two old gentlemen. I dressed in my best clothes, and I went to get Portia.

Before going to Portland Place, Portia and I talked about the job and the salary.

"Portia, you are so beautiful! When the two gentlemen meet you, they will give me any job and any salary I ask for."

"Henry, please remember that if we ask for too much, we will get nothing. Then what will happen to us?"

"Don't be afraid, Portia."

When we arrived, the same servant opened the door. There were the two old gentlemen having tea. They were surprised to see Portia. I introduced her to them.

Then I said, "Gentlemen, I am ready to report to you."

"We are pleased to hear this," said one gentleman. "Now we can decide the bet that my brother Abel and I made. If you won for me, you can have any job in my power. Do you have the million-dollar note?"

"Here it is, sir," and I gave it to him.

"I won!" he shouted. "Now what do you say, Abel?"

"I say he survived, and I lost twenty thousand dollars. I can't believe it!

"I have more to tell you," I said. "But, it's a long story. I'll tell you another time. For now, look at this."

"What! A Certificate of Deposit for $200,000. Is it yours?"

"It's mine. I earned it by using the banknote you lent me for a month."

"This is astonishing! I can't believe it."

Portia looked at me with surprise and said, "Henry, is that really your money? You didn't tell me the truth."

"No, I didn't. But, I know you'll forgive me."

"Don't be so sure! You told me a lie, Henry."

"Dearest Portia, it was only for fun. Come, let's go now."

"But, wait, wait!" my gentleman said. "I want to give you the job and the salary you choose."

"Thank you, thank you with all my heart. But I don't want the job."

"Henry, you didn't thank the good gentleman in the right way. Can I do it for you?" Portia said.

"Of course you can, my dear."

Portia walked to my gentleman, sat on his lap and kissed him on the mouth.

Then the two old gentlemen shouted and laughed. I was amazed. What was happening?

"Papa," said Portia, "Henry doesn't want your job. I feel very hurt."

"Darling, is that your father?" I asked.

"Yes, he's my stepfather, a dear man. Now do you understand why I laughed when you told me your story?"

"My dearest sir," I said, "I want to take back what I said. There is a job that I want."

"Tell me!"

"I want the job of son-in-law."

"Well, well, well. But you were never a son-in-law before. Do you know how to do this job?"

"Try me, please! Try me for thirty or forty years, and if—"

"Oh, all right. Take her!"

Were Portia and I happy? There aren't enough words in the dictionary to describe our happiness. When the Londoners heard the whole story of my adventures with the banknote, they talked of nothing else.

Portia's father took the banknote back to the Bank of England and cashed it. Then he gave us the cancelled banknote as a wedding present. We put it in a picture frame and hung it on the wall in our new home.

And so I always say, “Yes, it’s a million-dollar banknote, but it only bought one thing in its life; the most valuable thing in the world—Portia!”

www.ingramcontent.com/pod-product-compliance
Lightning Source LLC
Chambersburg PA
CBHW031956040826
48979CB00041B/181

9781479407071